Axolotl feels fed up.

I wish I wasn't one!

Just then, she spots an old gold
bottle lying on the sand.

She pulls the stopper...
with a

POP!

...it comes out in her hand!

Swirls of twirling wispy mist
curl around the lake.

"Oh no!" she cries.
"What have I done?
Was that a big mistake?"

She blinks
her eyes.

To her surprise, *a genie* has appeared!

He winks and smiles and all the while
he strokes his pointy beard.

You summoned me.
How can I help?

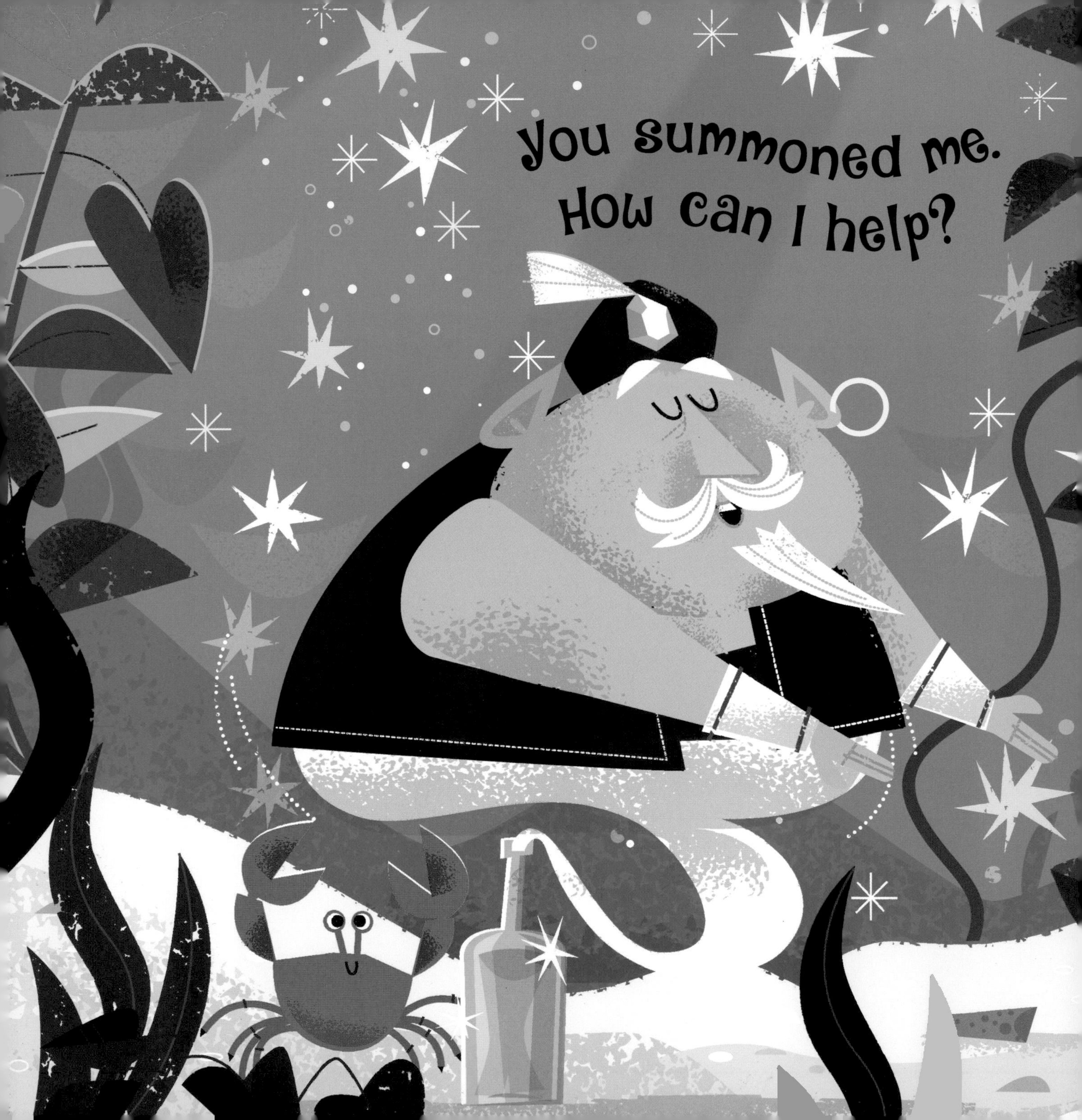

"The trouble is, you see, my life is dull. It's lonely. Oh, I don't like being me."

The genie makes a shower of stars.
He shakes and shouts out, "BINGO!"

Axolotl changes shape.
Now she's a flamingo!

"Thank you, Genie," she begins.

But then she starts to frown.

"I don't like standing on one leg.
I just keep falling down!"

"More magic!" cries the genie,
with a twinkle. "This is fab!"

"I don't like walking sideways
so I cannot be a crab."

The genie sighs and tries again.
"Please work this time," he begs.

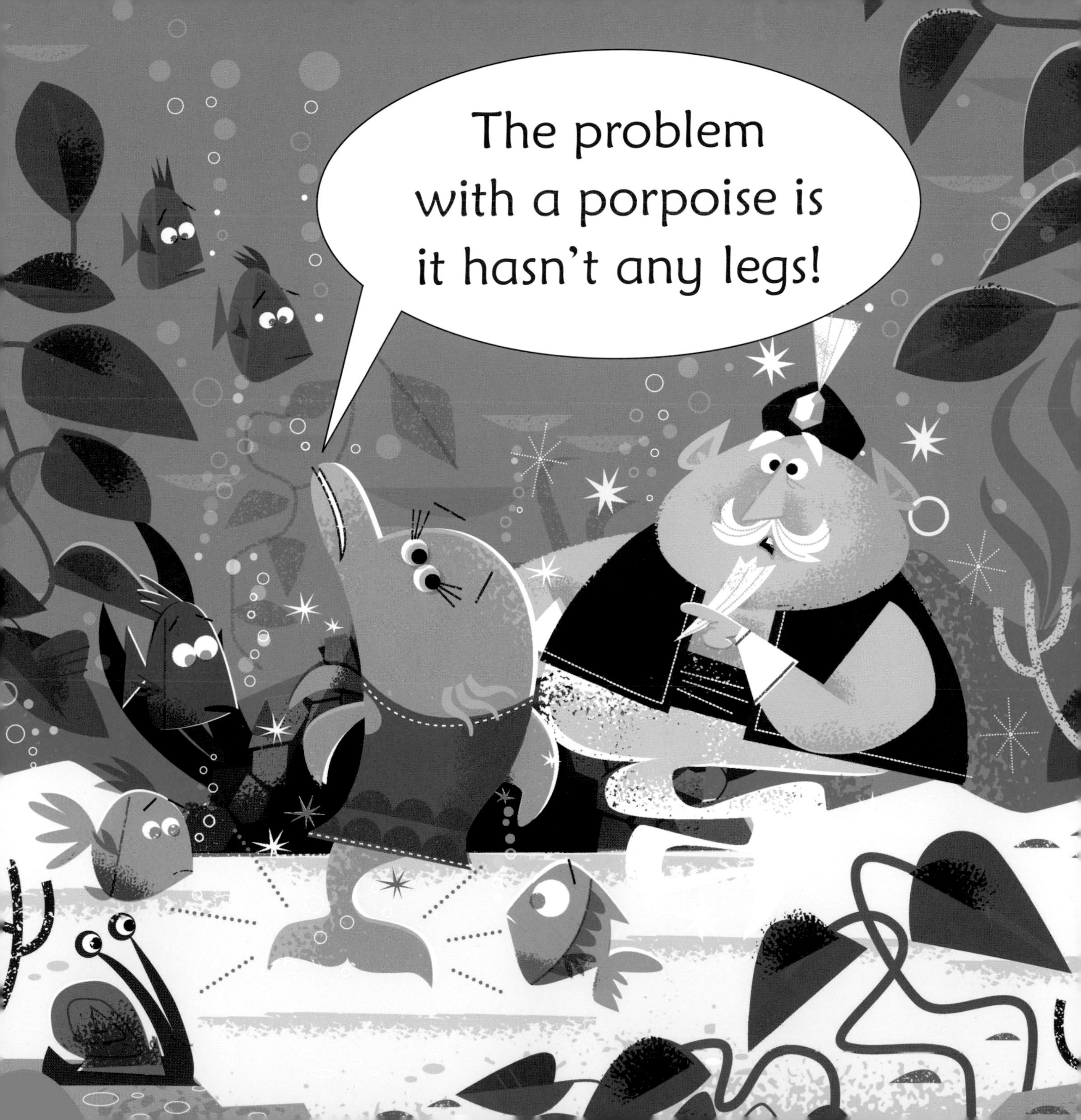
The problem with a porpoise is it hasn't any legs!

The genie thinks, "Things do look bleak."
At last, he gives a shriek.

"You simply need a friend...

...and then, some games
of hide-and-seek!"

About phonics

Phonics is a method of teaching reading which is used extensively in today's schools. At its heart is an emphasis on identifying the *sounds* of letters, or combinations of letters, that are then put together to make words. These sounds are known as phonemes.

Starting to read

Learning to read is an important milestone for any child. The process can begin well before children start to learn letters and put them together to read words. The sooner children can discover books and enjoy stories and language, the better they will be prepared for reading themselves, first with the help of an adult and then independently.

You can find out more about phonics on the Usborne Very First Reading website, **www.usborne.com/veryfirstreading** (US readers go to **www.veryfirstreading.com**). Click on the **Parents** tab at the top of the page, then scroll down and click on **About synthetic phonics**.

Phonemic awareness

An important early stage in pre-reading and early reading is developing phonemic awareness: that is, listening out for the sounds within words. Rhymes, rhyming stories and alliteration are excellent ways of encouraging phonemic awareness.

In this story, your child will soon identify the *o* sound, as in **lot** and **bottle**. Look out, too, for rhymes such as **lake** – **mistake** and **appeared** – **beard**.

Hearing your child read

If your child is reading a story to you, don't rush to correct mistakes, but be ready to prompt or guide if he or she is struggling. Above all, do give plenty of praise and encouragement.

About axolotls

Axolotls are real creatures. They live in just one lake in Mexico, Central America, but there are hardly any left in the wild. We have selected some websites you can visit with your child to find out more about axolotls. For links to these sites, go to www.usborne.com/quicklinks and type in axolotl.

Usborne Publishing is not responsible for the availability or content of any website other than its own.

Edited by Jenny Tyler   Designed by Sam Whibley
Reading consultants: Alison Kelly and Anne Washtell

First published in 2019 by Usborne Publishing Ltd., Usborne House, 83-85 Saffron Hill, London EC1N 8RT, England. www.usborne.com Copyright © 2019 Usborne Publishing Ltd.